Muggie Maggie

by Beverly Cleary
illustrated by Kay Life

Book Guide

SCHOLASTIC
LITERACY
PLACE®

WHAT'S NEW?
Grade 3, Unit 1

Cover from MUGGIE MAGGIE by Beverly Cleary, illustrated by Kay Life. Illustration copyright © 1990 by William Morrow & Company, Inc. Reprinted by permission of William Morrow & Company, Inc. Photograph of Beverly Cleary © Margaret Miller

Excepting those portions intended for classroom use, no part of this publication may be reproduced in whole or in part, or stored in a retrieval system, or transmitted in any form or by any means, electronic, mechanical, photocopying, recording, or otherwise, without written permission of the publisher.

For information regarding permission, write to Scholastic Inc., Instructional Publishing Group, 555 Broadway, New York, NY 10012. Scholastic Inc. grants teachers who have purchased *Scholastic Literacy Place* permission to reproduce from this book those pages intended for use in their classrooms. Notice of copyright must appear on all copies of copyrighted materials.

Copyright © 1996 Scholastic Inc.   All rights reserved.   Published by Scholastic Inc.   Printed in the U.S.A.

ISBN 0-590-53697-4

4 5 6 7 8 9 10   16   03 02 01 00 99 98 97

Contents

Dear Teacher,

Muggie Maggie is a funny look at a common third grade problem. Learning cursive writing is a challenge for many students. Through their reading and book conversations students will come to appreciate how one independent girl finds her own way to deal with change.

Overview

TEACHING OPTIONS

There are many ways that students can read and enjoy *Muggie Maggie*.

◆ Almost **all students** can benefit from having all or part of the book **read aloud** to help them appreciate the humor and true-to-life details in the story.

◆ A four-session plan that uses the **key strategy of Theme** balances **teacher guidance** with **demonstrating independence**. This option has students read portions of the book on their own, and then participate in teacher-led discussion to stimulate **meaningful conversation** and **comprehension**. See **Reading the Book** pages 6–10.

◆ **Cooperative groups** may work together to form **Literature Circles**. A blackline master is provided on page 11 to help students run their own successful Literature Circles.

◆ The blackline master on page 11 may also be adapted for use by students who are reading the book in **pairs** or **reading independently**.

◆ Introducing the Book, Assess Comprehension, Writing, Activities, and the Story Organizer are features of this guide that may be used with **all students** regardless of the reading options they choose.

CONNECT TO SOURCEBOOK

Resources in the ***What's New?* Teacher's SourceBook**, such as lessons relating to the **key strategy of Theme**, may also be adapted for use with *Muggie Maggie*. In addition, each plan in the *What's New?* Teacher's Sourcebook includes specific suggestions for **linking *Muggie Maggie* to the SourceBook literature**. Detailed suggestions are provided on pages **T76, T120,** and **T211** of the Teacher's SourceBook and on page **12** of this guide. Additional suggestions appear on pages T39, T157, and T245 of the Teacher's SourceBook.

JOURNAL WRITING

Throughout *Literacy Place*, students are encouraged to use journal writing to record their observations about what they read, note new vocabulary, and express their imaginations. Through journal writing, students also relate what they read to their own lives and develop the skills to assess their strengths and weaknesses as readers.

Within this guide, prompts for journal writing may be found on pages 4, 5, 7, 8, 9, 10, 11, 13, and 16.

PORTFOLIO ASSESSMENT

This guide offers a number of opportunities for portfolio assessment of both reading and writing.

WRITING
See pages
13, 14–15, 16.

READING
See pages
12–13, 16.

Introducing the Book

CREATE INTEREST

Print the following puzzle on the chalkboard:

A	EF	HI	KLMN		T	VWXY
	BCD	G	J	OPQRS	U	

Point out that all the letters of the alphabet except *Z* are shown. Does *Z* go above or below the line? To solve the puzzle, students need to figure out why the letters have been placed in these two different groups. Give this hint, if necessary: Study the shape of the letters. (Answer: *Z* goes above, because those letters have straight lines only; the letters below have curves.)

Display the cover of the book and invite students to read to find out why a young girl named Maggie would have a bit of trouble with a puzzle like the one above. Suggest that students who already know the story reread to learn more about Maggie's feelings and how they change.

BUILD BACKGROUND

Write your name on the chalkboard in both cursive script and in print. Have students describe how the two names look different. (In cursive, the letters are looped and connected.) Explain that the first writing is **cursive** and the second is **print.** Invite volunteers to come to the chalkboard and write their names in print and in cursive. Which is easier to do? Why? Explain that in the book students will read, the main character doesn't want to learn cursive writing.

DEVELOP VOCABULARY

Strategy: Knowledge Rating

Explain to students that *Muggie Maggie* contains many interesting words that vividly describe people's actions. Read aloud the vocabulary words and call on volunteers to define each word. Reinforce each definition by writing it and the word on the chalkboard.

Personal Word List Encourage students to look for more interesting words as they read *Muggie Maggie.* Suggest that in addition to looking for more action words, they can also look for other kinds of words, such as words that describe feelings or compound words. They can keep separate lists for each category of words.

Vocabulary
Organizing Concept: Action Words

burst: come in quickly (p. 2)

chasing: running after (p. 4)

dodging: getting out of the way; avoiding (p. 4)

tousled: curly; messed up (p. 7)

struggled: fought against (p. 15)

whispered: spoke quietly (p. 36)

rumpled: petted; touched affectionately (p. 43)

scrunched: pulled together (p. 44)

murmured: spoke in a low voice (p. 64)

PREVIEW AND PREDICT

Determine the Genre: Display the front cover of *Muggie Maggie* and invite students to guess if the book is fiction or nonfiction.

◆ **Does *Muggie Maggie* sound like a real name? What kind of books does Beverly Cleary usually write?**

◆ **Read the dedication of *Muggie Maggie*: "To a third-grade girl who wondered why no one ever wrote a book to help third graders read cursive writing."**

◆ **Based on these clues, what kind of book do you think this is? Why?**

Students may record their predictions and questions in their Journals. As they read they can verify or revise their predictions to see if the book is answering their questions.

ASSESSMENT

As students read the book, notice how they:

✔ make connections with the **theme** of how new experiences and new challenges are a part of life.

✔ use the **key strategy** of Theme.

✔ recognize how the strategies of **Comparing and Contrasting Information** and **Identifying Cause and Effect Relationships** can enhance their understanding of the book.

Reading On Students who are reading the book independently may read at their own pace. Other students may go on to read pages 1–20 of the book.

Meet the Author

Until third grade, Beverly Cleary didn't think reading was fun. She felt books were boring. But then she discovered a story "in which something happened." It excited her so much, she decided to write children's books herself. She has written dozens of books for children and won many awards, including the Newbery Medal for *Dear Mr. Henshaw*, two Newbery Honors, the ALA Laura Ingalls Wilder Award, and *School Library Journal* "Best Book" citations. *Muggie Maggie* was named an IRA-CBC "Children's Choice" selection, as are many of her books, reflecting her popularity with young readers. Recently, a sculpture garden populated by characters from her books was opened in her childhood neighborhood in Oregon, in which she has set so many of her stories.

MORE BEVERLY CLEARY

Henry and Beezus
by Beverly Cleary
Henry, with Beezus' aid, wants to find a way to get a bicycle—and in her first appearance in a Beverly Cleary book, Ramona tags along.

Henry Huggins
by Beverly Cleary
Henry Huggins and his dog Ribsy are introduced in this popular novel, Cleary's first published work. (Available in Spanish)

Ramona and Her Father
by Beverly Cleary
Ramona's father loses his job, and Ramona helps as only she can, in this Newbery Honor Book. (Available in Spanish)

Reading the Book

SESSION 1

After Pages 1-20

Synopsis After her first day in third grade, Maggie Schultz tells her parents that she doesn't want to learn cursive handwriting. She is happy typing on a computer. Back in school, Maggie refuses to practice making loops and lines. At home she tells her parents that they don't follow the cursive rules her teacher has explained.

 LAUNCH THE KEY STRATEGY

THEME

THINK ALOUD Most fictional stories are written with a theme, or message, in mind. Authors inform readers of their theme partly through the words and actions of their characters. That's one good reason it's important to pay close attention to what the characters are doing and saying, and what happens to them, while you're reading. As I focus on Maggie, I'll try to figure out the theme, or message, that the author is trying to tell me.

COMPREHENSION CHECK

What do you think of the book so far? (Respond to Literature)

Maggie doesn't seem to want to learn cursive writing. Based on her actions, what might be the theme the author will explore in this story? (Key Strategy: Theme) *The theme of the story will probably have something to do with learning something new.*

Summarize what happens when Maggie starts third grade. (Summarize) *She learns that she will learn cursive writing. When she comes home and tells her parents, she is disappointed by their reactions and decides she will not learn cursive. At school, she draws swooping lines instead of trying to write letters, and at home she criticizes her parents' writing.*

Maggie insists that she does not need to learn cursive writing, despite all the reasons her parents give her to learn it. What does Maggie's father mean when he calls her a "contrary kid"? (Context Clues) *He means she sometimes does the opposite of what she's asked to do.*

Do you think that Maggie should have to learn cursive writing? Why? (Make Judgments) *Possible answers: No, because she can use a computer, which is more advanced. Yes, because everyone else is learning cursive.*

Why do you think Maggie tells her parents that their cursive writing is wrong? (Make Inferences) *She may be trying to show that she does understand cursive, even though she won't use it.*

What do you think will happen to Maggie when she returns to school? (Make Predictions) *Possible answers: Mrs. Leeper will make her stay after school for a talk. Mrs. Leeper will call Maggie's parents.*

 Maggie thinks that cursive is hard to learn. Write about a school subject you once had a hard time with. Tell what you did to try to solve the problem.

Reading On In the next part of the book, pages 21–36, Maggie returns to school. Ask students to predict whether or not she will now start to learn cursive. Or, have students set their own purposes for reading.

EXTRA HELP Make sure students understand who the cast of characters are in this story and what their relationships are to Maggie. Invite them to list each character and describe his or her relationship to Maggie. **(Take Notes)**

ACCESS Have students assume the roles of story characters and read aloud the dialogue portions of the story, using their actions and words to portray character. Other students can serve as narrators who read text that is not dialogue. **(Role-play)**

Reading the Book

Synopsis   Maggie writes cursive in class but purposely makes it sloppy, "like a grown-up." Mrs. Leeper talks to Maggie's mother, and Maggie is sent to the principal and school psychologist. At home, Mr. Schultz bars Maggie from using the computer in an attempt to motivate her to work on her cursive writing. In class, students disagree on whether Maggie is brave or stupid. She is teased with the nickname "Muggie Maggie" after writing the *a* in her name as a *u*.

COMPREHENSION CHECK

What is the funniest thing that happened in this part of the story? (Respond to Literature)

What happens to Maggie after she refuses to write cursive neatly? (Summarize) *Mrs. Leeper calls in Mrs. Schultz for a talk. Maggie is sent to the principal and later the school psychologist. Mr. Schultz says Maggie can't use the computer anymore.*

What do Maggie's classmates think of her behavior? (Compare/Contrast) *All the students find it interesting. Some students think Maggie is being very foolish, while others think she is being very brave.*

MINI-LESSON

Why do you think Maggie insists on not cooperating in class? (Make Inferences) *She has gone this far, and to back down now would make her look foolish. She enjoys disagreeing with whatever she is asked to do.*

What is Beverly Cleary's theme, based on what Maggie does and what happens to her in this part of the book? (Key Strategy: Theme) *Sometimes people don't want to learn something new, which can make life difficult for them.*

JOURNAL Even though she knows she probably should, Maggie doesn't want to learn cursive. Have you, or someone you know, ever not wanted to do something that you should do? What was it? What caused you to do it?

Reading On   Before they begin reading the next part of the book, pages 37–51, ask children to predict if Maggie will keep up her "revolt." Students may read to answer this question or set their own purposes for reading.

MINI-LESSON

COMPARE/CONTRAST

THINK ALOUD When I read a story, I like to think about the characters. Characters can be similar in some ways. But in other ways, characters can be different. I compare to find similarities. I contrast to find differences. For example, in the book I can compare Maggie to Courtney and Kelly, who sit next to her. All of them are bothered by Kirby pushing the table. I can contrast Maggie with the two other girls by the way they react. Maggie pushes the table back; Kelly and Courtney at first say nothing and then ask the teacher for help.

APPLY Have students compare and contrast other characters in the story, such as other classmates or the adults in the book.

Synopsis Maggie receives a pen from her father's secretary, Ms. Madden. Her printed thank-you is sloppy, however, and Ms. Madden asks why she didn't copy it over. Maggie feels bad. In class she is appointed message monitor, but is upset to discover she is unable to read the cursive writing in the notes she delivers.

COMPREHENSION CHECK

What was the most surprising thing that happened in this part of the book? (Respond to Literature)

What two problems does Maggie have because she can't read or write cursive? (Problem/Solution) *She prints a thank-you note to Mrs. Madden, and she can't read the cursive her teacher uses on the board and in messages.*

How do you think Maggie feels about not being able to read cursive? Why does she feel that way? (Make Inferences) *She feels upset because she lacks a skill that other students in the class have already learned.*

What causes Maggie to suddenly find cursive interesting? (Cause/Effect) *She realizes that without being able to read cursive, she cannot read Mrs. Leeper's messages, or what she writes on the board.* `MINI-LESSON`

How do you think Maggie's position as message monitor reflects the theme of the book? (Key Strategy: Theme) *She finds that she has a reason to learn something new.*

How important do you think it is to know cursive writing? Explain your own point of view.

Reading On As they read on, in pages 52–70, ask students to predict what will happen to Maggie at the end of the story. Invite them to find out if their predictions are correct, or to set their own purposes for reading.

Cause	Effect
Maggie doesn't study cursive.	Maggie can't read cursive.

MINI-LESSON

CAUSE/EFFECT

TEACH/MODEL As I read a story, I notice that many things happen. There is usually a good reason why something happens. The reason is called the cause. What happens as a result is called the effect. For example, in Chapter 6, Maggie suddenly discovers she can't read cursive. Yet the other students in class are able to. What is the reason, or cause, for that? I know that all along, Maggie hasn't been studying her cursive lessons. The other children have. The cause is that Maggie hasn't studied. The effect is that she now can't read cursive.

APPLY Have students identify other causes and effects in the book and write them in a chart like the one shown on this page.

Reading the Book

SUPPORTING ALL LEARNERS

 EXTRA HELP Ask students to explain the ending of the story. Make sure they understand the real reason why Maggie was appointed message monitor. Also, have them explain why Maggie changes her thinking about cursive writing. **(Analyze)**

CHALLENGE Have students compose a note that Maggie might write to Mrs. Leeper, explaining how she feels about everything that has happened. **(Retell)**

SESSION 4
After Pages 52–70

Synopsis Maggie continues to deliver messages in school, but grows increasingly frustrated that she can't read the contents. She spends the next weekend at home studying and practicing cursive writing. Back in school, she discovers that she is now able to read cursive, and that her job as message monitor was meant to motivate her to learn.

COMPREHENSION CHECK

How do you feel about Maggie now that you've finished the book? Did your feelings about her change? Explain. (Respond to Literature)

How does Maggie solve her problem of not being able to read cursive writing? (Problem/Solution) *She spends an entire weekend studying cursive and practicing her writing until it is readable.*

Why does Mrs. Leeper say, "I don't think we need a message monitor anymore"? (Draw Conclusions) *The reason for making Maggie monitor was to encourage her to read cursive. Now that she's learned, her job is no longer needed.*

How is Maggie different at the end of the story? (Compare/Contrast) *She is now able to read and write cursive, and she is happier in class.*

Do you think Mrs. Leeper's plan for getting Maggie to learn cursive was a good one? Why or why not? (Make Judgments) *Possible answers: Yes, because it motivated Maggie to learn. No, because it took her out of the classroom a lot.*

How would you state the theme of this book? (Key Strategy: Theme) *Possible theme statements: It is important to be open to new experiences and new skills. Sometimes the reasons for learning something is not always immediately clear. Students sometimes have a hard time learning new subjects.*

 For Maggie, learning cursive writing was a big accomplishment. In your Journal write about something you have learned in school this year that you think is especially valuable.

Name

Literature Circles

Use these cards to help you as you read and discuss *Muggie Maggie.*
Record your ideas and answers in your Journal as you read.

SESSION 1
Pages 1-20

TALK ABOUT IT With your group, discuss the ways that Maggie's class is alike and different from your own. Look back at the book and write down quotes that describe the class or the people in it. Share these with the group. Would you want to be in this class?

SESSION 2
Pages 21-36

TALK ABOUT IT How does Mrs. Leeper try to handle the problem of getting Maggie to learn cursive writing? Go back to the book and list the steps she takes. Tell what happens in each case. Then share your notes with others.

SESSION 3
Pages 37-51

TALK ABOUT IT After Maggie writes a sloppy thank-you note for the new pen, Ms. Madden asks why she didn't copy it over neatly. With a partner, discuss what you think of Ms. Madden's answer. How does it make Maggie feel? Why do you think Mrs. Madden criticizes Maggie? Share your views with the rest of the class.

SESSION 4
Pages 52-70

TALK ABOUT IT How does Maggie feel about not being able to read the notes she delivers? Discuss with the group how Maggie feels when she discovers the notes are all about her. If you were Maggie, would you feel angry? foolish? confused? Explain your answer.

Copyright © 1996 Scholastic Inc.

Assess Comprehension

REFLECT AND RESPOND

What discoveries about the importance of new experiences did you get from *Muggie Maggie*? (✔ Theme Connection)

What do you think is the theme of this book? Give details from the story that support your ideas about the theme. (✔ Key Strategy: Theme)

How are Maggie's mother and her teacher alike? How are they different? (✔ Compare/Contrast)

What causes Maggie to change her views about cursive writing? (✔ Cause/Effect)

STORY ORGANIZER

Copy and distribute the Story Organizer on page 16 of this guide. Invite students to complete this page on their own. Encourage them to share their completed work by comparing their answers with those of other students.

READ CRITICALLY ACROSS TEXTS: CONNECT TO THE SOURCEBOOK

Ramona Forever

◆ Ask students to imagine that Ramona and Maggie are best friends, who leave school to walk home together. What would these two Beverly Cleary characters say and do together?

How My Family Lives in America

◆ What advice would April give to Maggie about learning a new skill? After imagining that the two girls are pen pals, invite students to write a letter from April to Maggie explaining why it might be important to learn cursive writing.

On the Pampas

◆ Encourage students to compare and contrast Maggie with the girl from *On the Pampas*. In what different ways did they react to new experiences? Suggest that students create a chart in which they record their comparisons of the two girls.

A Topic for Conversation

LEARNING NEW THINGS

People respond to new things in different ways. Many good books show how characters respond to changes. In *Muggie Maggie*, Maggie was easily discouraged as she attempted to learn cursive. She decided she would not learn it. Should she have responded differently? Invite all those who have read *Muggie Maggie* to discuss this question.

POSSIBLE ANSWERS:

Yes, because she would have to learn cursive, and she might as well get started.

Yes, because her parents and teacher wanted her to, and they knew what was best for her.

No, because she needed time to find a reason of her own to learn cursive.

No, because she already knew how to print and to use the computer.

IDEA FILE

Vocabulary

Have students use the vocabulary words and their personal word lists in a story of their own about a character learning a new skill. Encourage students to base their stories on an experience they themselves had. Is there anything about how they acted that they would change?

Ask the Author

What would students like to ask Beverly Cleary about *Muggie Maggie*? They might be interested in how the author creates the characters in her stories. Are they based on real people she has known? Encourage students to write their ideas and questions in their Journals.

Thank-You Letter

Have students use the computer to write another letter from Maggie to Ms. Madden, her father's secretary, thanking her for all the gifts she has given her. Students can also add a postscript—in cursive—explaining how they now know how to write in cursive script. Students can choose a special letterhead from the computer file for their letters.

Homework

Ask students to interview a parent or other relative about a new skill they learned. Students should ask whether learning the new skill was easy or hard and whether their interview subject wanted to learn the new skill at first. Then have students use their interview notes to write a paragraph in which they describe the experience they were told about in their interview.

Writing With an Alphabet Writing is not always done with a short alphabet like the Roman alphabet we use or the Cyrillic alphabet used for Russian. Chinese is written with many different characters, thousands in all, each representing a different word, idea, or sound. The ancient Egyptians created a picture writing called hieroglyphics, which you can see on mummies and carvings in the pyramids. Each hieroglyphic stood for a word or a syllable. Gradually, different cultures in the Middle East developed an alphabet in which the sign stood for sounds. The Greeks and Romans later developed this into the alphabet we use today.

ASSESSMENT

The checked questions on page 12 help assess students' understanding of:

✔ the **theme** of responding to new experiences.

✔ the **key strategy** of Theme.

✔ how the **strategies** of **Compare/Contrast** and **Cause/Effect** enhance their understanding of the book.

You may also wish to review and discuss selected students' completed Story Organizers.

Listen to Students Read Ask selected students to find a place in the book that described feelings they themselves have experienced. You may wish to tape-record students as they read the section aloud.

Students may add their recordings, copies of favorite Journal entries, their completed Story Organizer, and other completed assignments to their Literacy Portfolios.

Writing

In the Author's Words

"I started out feeling that writers wrote on the typewriter, but I soon found that thinking confused my typing, which was never good. I now write in cheap pen on legal paper, and then I type my work—badly—so that I can see what it looks like, and I revise that....I don't know about computers. I have a friend who used to write short, witty letters. Then she bought a word processor. The last letter I got was one yard long, and it was not very interesting."

Beverly Cleary
from Contemporary Authors

WRITING PROMPTS

Writer's Style: Details

Beverly Cleary brings her characters to life through carefully selected details, which reveal their feelings as they speak to each other. Invite students to use the conversation between Maggie and Mr. Galloway on pages 25–27 as a model to help them create a conversation (or dialogue) between two characters. After students have created their first drafts, encourage them to revise the conversations. Remind them to use quotations marks when a character is speaking, to use details that make it clear which character it is, and how that character feels.

Speech

Have students imagine that Mrs. Leeper asked Maggie to give a speech about why it is important to learn cursive writing. Invite students to step into the character of Maggie and write the speech. They should make a list of reasons before they write. Encourage students to read aloud their first drafts to another student, making notes about any parts they would like to change. Students may present their final speeches to the class.

Fiction: Character Sketch

Muggie Maggie is full of interesting characters. Have students select a character from the book and write a character sketch of that character: Maggie, her mother and father, Mrs. Leeper, the principal, or anyone else they especially liked. Suggest that students use a chart to make notes about their character, listing each character's special traits, before they begin writing their sketches.

Character _____
Important traits:
1 _____
2 _____
3 _____
4 _____
5 _____

Activities

INTEGRATING LANGUAGE ARTS
Writing/Speaking
Interview Tell students that they are being assigned to interview Maggie for the school newspaper. They should first make a list of questions they would like to ask. The questions could be about her schoolwork, friends, parents, dog, or other subjects they choose. Have students imagine and write down the answer that Maggie would give to each question. Partners can then rehearse the interview, with one student playing the interviewer and the other, Maggie. Invite students to perform their interviews for the class.

Speaking/Listening
Debate Have students consider whether computers will someday make it unnecessary to learn many things, including writing cursive (or even printing). They should prepare by listing what computers can/cannot replace now and in the future. They can begin their lists by using the ideas they find in the book, but encourage students to add their own ideas. Then have the class conduct a debate over the question of whether or not computers will make many skills unnecessary. Some students might enjoy being assigned to "cover" the debate as reporters. After the exchange of views is complete, the students who observed the proceedings can deliver television news reports in which they summarize the views given during the debate.

INTEGRATING THE CURRICULUM
The Arts
The passages in the book detailing Maggie's experiences as message monitor lend themselves to dramatization. Have students work in groups to stage a performance of this part of the book. Students can take the roles of Mrs. Leeper, Maggie, and the principal, writing dialogue for each, complete with stage directions that say how the character should act, what kind of movements they should make, and so on. Invite different groups to perform their scenes for the entire class.

Science
Computer Handbook Have students note that one of the reasons cursive writing is not used as much as it was in the past is because people are using computers more and more to do their writing. Have students research how computers are used, then prepare a handbook that will help people write on the computer. Students could include in their handbooks such information as how to turn the computer on and off, how to save and print what they've written, how to change mistakes, how to move text around, and any other features of the computers available to them.

Story Organizer

The theme is the idea about life that the author wants the reader to take away from a story. Complete the diagram below to tell about the theme of *Muggie Maggie*.

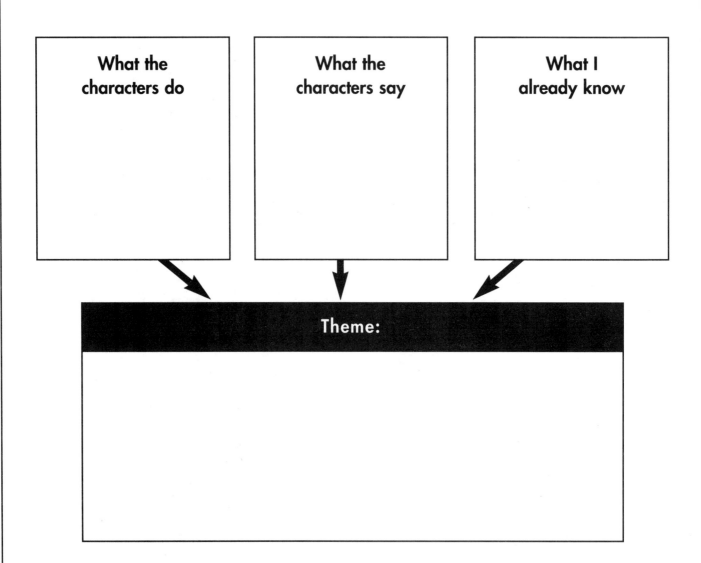

What the characters do	What the characters say	What I already know

Theme:

At the end of the book, Maggie thinks that perhaps she will someday decide not to write in cursive after all. How might learning a new skill be important, even if you decide not to use it? Write a few sentences to explain your answer.

Copyright © 1996 Scholastic Inc.